Mac the Knight

by Leslie McGuire

Illustrated by Thompson Bros.

Based on the books by Norman Bridwell

SCHOLASTIC INC.
New York   Toronto   London   Auckland   Sydney
Mexico City   New Delhi   Hong Kong   Buenos Aires

CLANK! BONK!
CLATTER! CLINK!

"What is all that noise?" asked Cleo. Clifford looked up just in time to see an odd pile of old tin cans go by.

"I know!" said T-Bone. "That's Mac!"

"That's right!" said Mac. "I am Mac the Knight. Do you want to be in my play?"

"Who wrote the play?" asked Cleo.

"I did," said Mac. "I am a knight who never gets things wrong. I save the pretty princess, too."

"Can I be the pretty princess?" asked Cleo.

"Yes," said Mac. "T-Bone can be the bad wizard, and Clifford can be the dragon who has her trapped in this tree!"

Mac started to wind a chain around Cleo, but his leg got stuck. Mac fell down on his knees.

CLATTER! CLANK! BONK! CLINK!

"This chain is too big," said Mac. "I have to use a rope." But Mac could not make a knot with all the cans on his paws.

"I will wrap it tight for you," said T-Bone.

"Now I will take this knife to cut the rope and save the pretty princess," said Mac. But Mac's knife was made of wood. The wood broke and knocked Mac on the wrist. CLONK! CLINK! BONK!

Cleo started to giggle.

"No giggling!" yelled Mac. "That will wreck my play!"

"I know," said Clifford. "The knight should wind Cleo's magic shawl around the mysterious wizard." But Mac's head got wrapped up in the shawl. CLINK! CLANK! CLONK! BONK!

Mac did not know
what to do.

"This play is turning out
all wrong," he said. "The
knight has not done one
thing right yet! All he
does is wreck things!"

"Don't be so sad," said
Clifford. "We can write a
new play!"

They helped Mac take off all the tin cans.

CLATTER! BONK! BONK! CLINK!

Then they sat down to write another play.

This play was about four smart dogs who make a magic race car out of tin cans. The car is so fast they win all the big racing prizes.

"Writing plays is fun!"
said Mac. "Let's write
another one."